Hungry as a Horse

A SIROCCO STORY

By Sibley Miller

Illustrated by Tara Larsen Chang and Jo Gershman

Feiwel and Friends

For Mose and Lewis—Sibley Miller

To the painters of Bumping Lake for warm
encouragement, sharp-eyed criticism, and fabulous meals
—Tara Larsen Chang and Jo Gershman

A FEIWEL AND FRIENDS BOOK
An Imprint of Macmillan

WIND DANCERS: HUNGRY AS A HORSE. Copyright © 2009
by Reeves International, Inc. All rights reserved. BREYER,
WIND DANCERS, and BREYER logos are trademarks and/or registered
trademarks of Reeves International, Inc. Printed in June 2011 in China by
Leo Paper, Heshan City, Dongguan City, Guangdong Province.
For information, address Feiwel and Friends,
175 Fifth Avenue, New York, N.Y. 10010.

Library of Congress Cataloging-in-Publication Data

Miller, Sibley.
Hungry as a horse : a Sirocco story / by Sibley Miller ; illustrated by
Tara Larsen Chang and Jo Gershman.
p. cm. — (Wind Dancers ; #8)
Summary: Sirocco wants to do most of the eating and none of the cooking,
but when he boasts that he could cook better than the three fillies working
together, Brisa, Kona, and Sumatra challenge him to a contest.
ISBN: 978-0-312-56403-2 (alk. paper)
[1. Cookery—Fiction. 2. Contests—Fiction. 3. Horses—Fiction.
4. Magic—Fiction.]
I. Chang, Tara Larsen, ill. II. Gershman, Jo, ill. III. Title.
PZ7.M63373Hun 2009   [Fic]—dc22   2009016142

Series editor, Susan Bishansky
Designed by Barbara Grzeslo
Feiwel and Friends logo designed by Filomena Tuosto

First Edition: 2009

3 5 7 9 10 8 6 4 2

mackids.com

CONTENTS

Meet the Wind Dancers

One day, a little girl named Leanna blows on a doozy of a dandelion. To her delight and surprise, four tiny horses spring from the puff of the dandelion seeds!

Four tiny horses with shiny manes and shimmery wings. Four magical horses who can fly!

Dancing on the wind, surrounded by magic halos, they are the Wind Dancers.

The leader of the quartet is **Kona**. She has a violet-black coat and vivid purple mane, and she flies inside a halo of magical flowers.

Brisa is as pretty as a tropical sunset with her coral-pink color and blonde mane and tail. Magical jewels make up Brisa's halo, and she likes to admire her gems (and herself) every time she looks in a mirror.

Sumatra is silvery blue with sea-green wings. Much like the ocean, she can shift from calm to stormy in a hurry! Her magical halo is made up of ribbons, which flutter and dance as she flies.

The fourth Wind Dancer is—surprise!—a colt. His name is Sirocco. He's a fiery gold, and he likes to go-go-go. Everywhere he goes, his magical halo of butterflies goes, too.

The tiny flying horses live together in the dandelion meadow in a lovely house carved out of the trunk of an apple tree. Every day, Leanna wishes she'll see the magical little horses again. (She's sure they're nearby, but she doesn't know they're invisible to people.) And the Wind Dancers get ready for their next adventure.

CHAPTER 1

If You Give a Horse a Muffin . . .

It was morning in the Wind Dancers' apple tree house, and that meant Sirocco was on clean-up duty from an apple muffin breakfast.

First, he took the breakfast dishes to the water trough and scrubbed them *splashily*. (Kona sighed good-naturedly and dried the floor with a dandelion fluff mop. Sirocco didn't notice.)

Then, Sirocco used his teeth to stack the breakfast plates on a shelf. (He *also* failed to spot Brisa straightening them into a neater, prettier stack.)

Finally, the golden colt blew all the crumbs off the table with a few gusts of hot breath. (And once again, he didn't have any idea that Sumatra had swept the crumbs from the floor with her pale green tail.)

With his chores finished, Sirocco blew his yellow-gold forelock out of his eyes and said, "*Whew!* What's on the menu for our mid-morning snack?"

Kona gaped.

Brisa gasped.

But Sumatra spoke up!

"Mid-morning snack?" she asked. "You still have apple muffin crumbs around your mouth from breakfast!"

"I *know*, but look at this kitchen!" Sirocco said. "It's sparkling! And all because of *my* hard work."

"Oh, *really*? *Your* hard work?" Sumatra asked dryly, while Brisa tittered and Kona rolled her coal-black eyes.

"Well, of course!" the clueless colt said innocently. "And hard work always makes me *extra* hungry!"

Then he turned to Kona.

"You know," he said generously, "I don't need something different for my snack. I'll just take a couple more of those yummy muffins you made for breakfast. We'll call it seconds."

"More like *fourths*!" Kona said. "Besides, there aren't any muffins *left* from breakfast. Not after you ate three whole ones already! You eat food as fast as I can make it."

"*Hmm,*" Sirocco said, pondering this problem. Then, his brown eyes lit up!

"I have a solution!" he said. "Sumatra and Brisa should help you more often with the cooking. Then you could make more food!"

The three fillies gaped at each other.

Brisa's always-sunny face clouded over.

Sumatra's eyes went from pale green to stormy turquoise.

And the flowers in Kona's magic halo—which usually bounced cheerfully around her—trembled in fury.

"I have a *better* solution," the violet-black Wind Dancer said to Sirocco through gritted teeth. "How about *you* start doing some cooking yourself?"

"*Me*?!" Sirocco squawked.

"Yes, you!" Brisa chimed.

"*Please*," Sirocco scoffed. He clopped his (not terribly clean) front hooves on the table. "Isn't it enough that I help with the cleaning up around here? I'm not going to *cook*, too. That's filly's work! I'm a *colt*!"

"Oh, he *didn't* just say that, did he?" Sumatra neighed to Brisa.

"He *did*!" Brisa gasped in disbelief.

Kona shook her head and looked to the heavens. Then she spoke to Sirocco with a quiet chill in her voice.

"If *that's* how you feel," she said to the suddenly nervous colt, "maybe you should go off and have your *own* adventure today. I'm sure whatever we fillies want to do would be too *girly* for you."

"Oh, come on!" Sirocco protested. "I didn't mean it like that."

"Then you *didn't* mean that cooking was 'filly's work'?" Kona asked.

"I just meant," Sirocco's eyes went shifty, as he searched for a way to get his hoof out of his mouth. "I just meant that you fillies cook so much *better* than me. For your *own* sakes, you should be the ones to do it!"

"I'm sure we could manage to choke down your cooking, *somehow*," Sumatra offered sweetly—while Kona snorted and Brisa bit her lip to keep from laughing.

Sirocco stared at his friends. He *knew* they were teasing him. They were trying to *make* him cook something.

And they probably wouldn't stop teasing him until he *did* cook something.

And then there was the matter of his hungry belly . . .

Grumble-grumble-groooowwwwwl.

The sounds of Sirocco's hunger were unmistakable.

"Oh, fine!" Sirocco blustered to the fillies. "You want me to cook, I'll cook! I just hope my food doesn't make you turn green!"

"That won't be a problem for *me*!" Sumatra giggled, tossing her sea-green mane.

"*Har, har, har,*" Sirocco said with an eye roll. Then he clopped over to the pantry and began to pull out whatever random foods he spotted—some honey, apples, a rutabaga or two, oats, barley, and cornmeal.

As he gazed at the ingredients, a flutter of fear replaced the hunger in his belly. He really had *no* idea what to do with them!

On the other hand, he *couldn't* back down from Kona's challenge! So—while the three amused fillies watched—Sirocco grabbed some wooden bowls and baking tins. He gripped a spoon between his teeth. And then he dove in.

Rutabaga peels and flour flew.

Barley skittered across the wood floor.

Honey dripped onto Sirocco's hair and cornmeal crunched beneath his hooves.

He chopped and diced. He stirred and sautéed. He kneaded and baked.

Finally—breathing heavily and shaking sweat off his brow—Sirocco presented his friends with a snack.

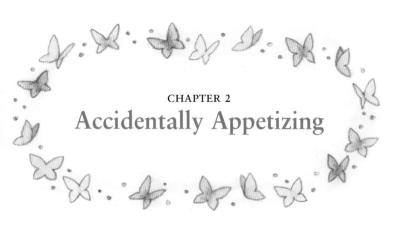

CHAPTER 2
Accidentally Appetizing

Brisa's eyes filled with fear as she took a tiny nibble of Sirocco's snack—a pan of mushy stuff topped with a sort of crumble.

But the filly didn't spit or gag or even grimace. She *smiled*!

"It's really yummy!" she rejoiced, taking another, and bigger, bite.

"*What?!*" Kona and Sumatra cried at the same time.

Nobody was more surprised than Sirocco himself! He edged the fillies out of the way and took a huge bite. Then he gasped as he tasted a pleasing crunch, a delicious sweetness, an aromatic fruitiness!

"Ew, Sirocco!" Brisa protested. "Don't gasp with your mouth full!"

"Full of *what* is what I want to know," Sumatra said, as she got her own blissful taste of the dish.

"Um, rutabagas, apples, oats, and some other crunchy stuff!" Sirocco listed, still stunned by the dish's success. He took another large, delicious bite. "Let's call it

Apple Rutabaga Crunch."

The colt's smile grew.

"No, scratch that," he said, tossing his gold mane proudly. "Let's call it *Sirocco's Awesome* Apple Rutabaga Crunch! Who knew that deep down, I was actually a brilliant chef?!"

Sirocco proved his point by taking another enormous bite of his amazing snack.

"Mmmm, *squish*, yum, yum, *chomp*," Sirocco moaned as he chewed with his mouth open again.

"I don't know which is more obnoxious," Sumatra said to Kona and Brisa. "Sirocco's table manners or his big head!"

"Oh, *please*," Kona said, taking her own bite of Crunch. "This yummy snack was clearly a case of beginner's luck."

"Luck, you say? No way!" Sirocco replied. "I *clearly* have a natural talent for cooking.

One that's been undiscovered until now!"

Sumatra snorted (even as she helped herself to another delicious morsel of Awesome Apple Rutabaga Crunch).

"Oh, you don't agree?" Sirocco challenged her. "How about we have a contest? A cook-off!"

"Ooh," Sumatra breathed to Kona and Brisa with a mischievous smile. "Imagine how satisfying it would be for one of us to beat the horseshoes off of Sirocco in this contest!"

Kona nodded eagerly and turned to the colt.

"You're on!" she said. "We'll each cook a dish and then decide whose is the best."

But Sirocco shook his head.

"Too easy," he scoffed. "I can beat all three of you *put together*."

Brisa sighed.

Kona seethed.

And Sumatra simmered.

The fillies barely had to glance at each other to agree to Sirocco's dare.

"You want three to one—us against you?" Kona asked the colt. "You've got it! The Great Wind Dancer Cook-Off begins *now*!"

CHAPTER 3
A Gourmet Goof

All the Wind Dancers could almost *taste* the sweetness of victory. And they couldn't *wait* to get started on their foodie adventure.

The three fillies put their noses together and began whispering about recipes and ingredients.

Sirocco overheard Sumatra suggest corn, and Kona ponder parsnips. Brisa was all about pretty, Pink Lady apples.

"Oh, *please*!" Sirocco sniffed to the fillies. "Those ingredients are so ordinary, so everyday, so . . . *horsy*! A truly great chef

20

cooks with strange spices, exotic vegetables, and fabulous fruits!"

"Well, then," Sumatra said snippily, "why don't *you* go off and find yourself some of those 'exotic' ingredients so *we* can get started on *our* cooking?"

"Gladly!" Sirocco declared with a smug grin. He neighed good-bye to his friends and fluttered out of the apple tree house.

Right away, he noticed something shimmering in the dandelion meadow just below him.

"Hmmm!" Sirocco murmured to himself. The curious colt couldn't help but swoop down for a look. And when he did, he happened upon a bustling family of grasshoppers!

Every one of the insects was munching happily on dandelion leaves.

Sirocco had blown on tons of dandelion puffs and admired hundreds of yellow dandelion blooms, but never *once* had he thought to taste the weeds' spiky leaves!

He took a big chomp out of a dandelion leaf. It was delicately bitter and subtly spicy—it was delicious!

"Who knew?" Sirocco said. Right away, he began using his teeth to pluck leaf after leaf from the meadow's many dandelions.

"A dandelion green salad is the *perfect* way to start the Cook-Off," Sirocco said to himself proudly. "After all, dandelions were the start of us Wind Dancers!"

Sirocco tied up a bunch of leaves with a long dandelion stem. Then he tucked the greens under the sash he wore around his neck.

"But now," Sirocco said to himself as he fluttered into the air, "my bitter salad needs something sweet. Any chef knows that in great food, balance is everything!"

But *what* sweet something should he get? He needed something way more fabulous and edgy than the Wind Dancers' usual apples, blackberries, and honey—

Honk! Honkhonkhonkhonk!

Sirocco was startled out of his pondering by a big V of geese flapping, honking, and grinning excitedly over his head.

"Hey, what's going on?" Sirocco called to the geese as they rushed past.

One goose slowed her flapping for a moment to scoff at Sirocco.

"Don't you know?" she asked in a high, squeaky honk. "The gooseberries are ripe! Every goose and gander around here is going to the feast."

"Gooseberries!" Sirocco said. "What are those?"

"Only the most succulent, *delicious* berry *ever*," the goose said.

"Then they're the *perfect* ingredient for my bitter dandelion green salad!" Sirocco exclaimed. "Lead the way, friend!"

Suddenly, the chatty goose balked.

"B-but," she protested, "they're *goose-*berries. *We* get first crack at them!"

"What?" Sirocco said. "That's no fair!"

"Welllllll," the goose glanced around sneakily, "I guess it's a free meadow. Just follow our V to the gooseberry bushes. But you didn't hear it from me!"

"Deal!" Sirocco said, cackling with satisfaction.

See? he told himself as he snuck behind another goose and coasted in its tailwind. *Only a great chef would go to such lengths to find his ingredients. Wait 'til the fillies taste my salad!*

Before Sirocco knew it, he found himself within a throng of geese, all nipping small, juicy, red berries from a thicket of spiky bushes.

He used his teeth to pluck two perfect gooseberries, and tucked them between his forelegs. He was just scoping around for more when he heard a loud honk right next to him.

It was loud *and* angry.

"What are *yooooou* doing here?" said this goose.

"Um," Sirocco said, "I'm gathering gooseberries, just like you?"

"But they're *goose*berries," the goose

honked. "*You're* no *goose*! You're a strange little *horse*!"

"I'm a chef!" Sirocco defended himself loudly. "Besides, it's a free meadow!"

Honk! Honkhonkhonkhonk!

Apparently, Sirocco had attracted the attention of several other geese, too.

Who will surely see things my way, right? Sirocco asked himself nervously.

Wrong!

"The *goose*berries are *ouuuuuurrrrs*!" the geese honked. They began to lunge at Sirocco!

"*Aigh!*" Sirocco neighed. Luckily, he was faster than the berry-stuffed geese and able to dart away.

"You're not very friendly, are you?" Sirocco scolded them. "Friends share!"

"*Ouuuuuuuurrrrs!*" the geese honked back. They began flapping into the air to chase him!

"I'm going to take these berries back to my kitchen if it's the last thing I do!" Sirocco shouted at the geese with a mischievous grin.

"*Ooouuuuurrrrss!*" the geese insisted.

Then they began flapping their wings harder. And faster. And the closer they got to Sirocco, the bigger they looked!

"*Wh-wh-whoa!*" Sirocco whinnied.

He had no choice but to flee!

CHAPTER 4

(Not So) Marvelous Mushrooms

Only by flying racehorse-fast did Sirocco escape the gooseberry-hogging geese. But escape he did! He ducked into the forest and hid between a couple of tree roots.

When he was sure the coast was clear, Sirocco cackled.

"Greedy geese!" he whinnied. "At least I still have my two perfect gooseberries!"

Sirocco looked triumphantly at his forelegs—and gasped!

"Oh, no!" he neighed. His berries were gone! All that was left of them was a smudge of red juice staining his white socks!

"I must have dropped them when I was escaping!" Sirocco cried. "I *can't* go back for them now!"

Sirocco slumped against his tree root in despair. But instead of feeling scratchy bark against his flank, he felt spongy, velvety smoothness!

"Huh?" Sirocco said.

He spun around to discover a slightly flattened . . . "Mushroom!" Sirocco cried.

The wide-brimmed fungus was a lovely tan color—and it was surrounded by at least a dozen more just like it.

"I can make a meal of wild mushrooms!" Sirocco exclaimed.

His lost berries forgotten, Sirocco plucked up three pretty mushrooms. Then he flitted along the forest floor, scanning every mossy log and stone for more.

It only took him a few minutes to spot some long-stemmed, cream-colored ones growing next to a creek!

"Hot dog!" Sirocco cried as he swooped down to add a few to his mushroom stash.

"Hot head is more like it!" said a squeaky

 voice behind Sirocco. The Wind Dancer colt whirled around and saw a brown field mouse looking at him skeptically.

"What do you mean, 'hot head'?" Sirocco demanded of the mouse.

"If you eat those mushrooms, you're going to get a bad fever!" the mouse squeaked matter-of-factly. "Probably a headache and bellyache, too. Or a whole lot worse! They're poisonous!"

"*Ack!*" Sirocco neighed, dropping all his mushrooms. "What am I going to do? How can I win a cooking contest with only a bunch of dandelion leaves?!"

"What? Do you think I have *all* the answers?" the mouse squeaked. He scampered off in a huff.

"Thanks for the mushroom tip!" Sirocco

whinnied weakly after the retreating mouse.

Then he sighed. "I might as well head home," he told himself, "and think about plan B."

But when Sirocco fluttered into the air, he realized something. He'd done so many twists and turns in his mushroom hunt that he'd gotten turned around! He didn't know which *way* home was!

"Where am I?" he neighed.

He began dashing through the woods in a panic. After a few minutes of flying turned up no sign of the dandelion meadow, Sirocco threw himself onto a tree branch.

"I'm stranded in the woods!" he gasped tragically. "Lost! Who *knows* how long it'll take me to find my way."

Grumble-rumble-grooooooowwwwwl!

Sirocco looked down at his belly. *It* was feeling miserable, too!

"Oh, no," Sirocco groaned. "I'm lost *and* hungry! What will I do?"

His desperate eyes fell on the dandelion leaf bundle tucked into his sash necklace.

"I have no choice!" Sirocco neighed dramatically. "I must eat to survive!"

With that, he messily devoured his spicy salad fixings.

"Whew," Sirocco sighed in relief. "I'm saved. For now . . ."

But he still had to find his way out of the woods! Sirocco flew upward a few feet. From there he spotted a break in the treetops—a window through which he could see blue sky, dazzling sunbeams and . . . a familiar-looking apple tree!

"Could it be?" Sirocco wondered. He raced through the branches and found himself fluttering above his very own dandelion meadow, near his very own apple tree house!

"Yessssss!" Sirocco whinnied—until he remembered he didn't have any ingredients for the Great Wind Dancer Cook-Off.

"Nooooooo!" Sirocco groaned, feeling foolish. "This couldn't get any worse!"

"Oh, it smells delicious, Kona!"

Sirocco jumped as Brisa's sweet chirpy voice floated out of the tree house's kitchen window. Then he groaned.

35

"I guess it *could* get worse," he whispered to himself. "Not only has my mission to find exotic ingredients failed, but I have to hear about how fabulous Kona's cooking is!"

He flew slowly down to the apple tree, cringing with every flutter of his wings. When he clopped into the kitchen, Kona was just pulling two beautiful—and indeed delicious-smelling—parsnip pies out of the oven.

"Don't look, don't look!" Brisa shrieked, cantering over to Sirocco and draping her thick blonde mane over his eyes. "We made these for the cook-off. We want you to be surprised!"

"Surprised?" Sumatra said. "Who cares if he's surprised? *I* just don't want him to steal our idea!"

"Oh, I'm sure Sirocco would never do that," Kona chided Sumatra gently.

"Yeah!" Sirocco declared proudly.

"Because *I* don't need to! I have a fabulous plan myself!"

"Oh, *really*?" Sumatra said skeptically.

While Sirocco stuck his pink tongue out at the green filly, Kona set one of her pies on the windowsill and put the other one in the Wind Dancers' picnic basket.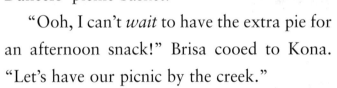

"Ooh, I can't *wait* to have the extra pie for an afternoon snack!" Brisa cooed to Kona. "Let's have our picnic by the creek."

Sirocco couldn't help but stare hungrily at the beautiful pie.

And he couldn't help but picture the three fillies lounging by the creek and munching their delicious snack—without him.

But then he imagined *himself*, doing a cloppity victory dance after winning the Great Wind Dancer Cook-Off. And that got him *right* back on his what-to-do track.

"Pie!" he said to his friends, snorting with disdain. "Was *that* the best you could come up with?"

"No," Sumatra said, flapping her ears indignantly. "I also found a *perfect* ear of corn in Leanna's garden. I'm going to do something magical with it!"

"And *I'm* going to cook something with a Pink Lady apple I found," Brisa piped up with a dreamy smile. "Something *pretty*!"

Sirocco made a big show of yawning.

"Corn and apples," he said sarcastically. *"How exciting!"*

"Okay, big talker!" Kona challenged Sirocco. "Tell us how *your* ingredient hunt went. Did you find anything 'exotic'?"

"Of course I did!" Sirocco declared automatically. "I found foods you've never even *heard* of!"

And he wasn't fibbing. His mushrooms, gooseberries, and dandelion greens *would* have been fabulous finds—if they  hadn't been poisonous, lost, and eaten!

"So," Sumatra asked, looking pointedly at Sirocco's empty forelegs and sash necklace, *"what* exactly did you get?"

"Well . . . well," Sirocco stammered, "a great chef never tells! I've stashed away my ingredients for later. You'll just have to wait for my magnificent meal to find out!"

"Okay," Brisa said with a smile and a shrug. "Do you want to join us for a snack in the meantime?"

Sirocco sniffed—taking in the yummy scent of Kona's pie as he did.

Which only made him more hungry. Not to mention cranky!

"Wouldn't you like *that*?" Sirocco blurted. "Ply me with lunch and pry my cooking secrets out of me? I don't *think* so!"

Sirocco was so busy acting mad, he didn't spot the fillies grinning at one another.

"Now if you'll excuse me," the great chef said self-importantly, "*I* have more cooking prep to do!"

With that, he darted away.

CHAPTER 5

Food Fit for a . . . Squirrel?

After leaving the fillies in a huff, Sirocco flew aimlessly above the dandelion meadow. Without his great ingredients, he didn't know *how* he was going to win the Great Wind Dancer Cook-Off!

To cheer himself up, he did a few loop-de-loops and back-flips.

And *that's* when he suddenly realized something!

"Wait a minute!" he said to himself. "I don't need exotic ingredients to win the Cook-Off! This morning, after all, I made my

Awesome Apple Rutabaga Cunch with random horsy stuff I found in the pantry. I just need to work the same magic again! And with my natural talent, I'm sure I will."

Hooray! Sirocco tossed his mane in a way that he hoped made him look like a proud chef.

He was just about to head back home to get cooking when he spotted a familiar yellow house nearby. The colt grinned. That was Leanna's farmhouse! He'd flown there without even being aware of it.

"Maybe before I get to cooking," Sirocco proposed to himself, "I'll just stop and pay Leanna a little visit."

He *was* a tiny bit lonely, after all.

Leanna's kitchen window was open, so Sirocco zipped over to peek inside.

Then, he gasped in delight.

Clearly, the Wind Dancers weren't the *only* ones cooking today! Leanna and her little

sister, Sara, were standing in front of a big mixing bowl and an open cookbook. They were wearing too-big aprons, and they were surrounded by canisters of oats, flour, and sugar, a box of raisins, a bottle of vanilla, and other yummy-looking ingredients.

"These are going to be the *best* cookies at our school bake sale," Leanna assured her sister with a grin.

"Well, *yeah*," Sara agreed. She popped a raisin into her mouth.

"Now *that's* what I call cooking!" Sirocco said, his mouth watering.

But as he watched the girls carefully read their recipe, measure and mix ingredients, then spoon balls of cookie dough onto a baking sheet, Sirocco felt his tail droop and his ears sag. The butterflies in his magic halo grew sad, too.

"That looks pretty complicated," the colt whispered to himself in a trembly voice. "How is *anybody* supposed to keep all those ingredients *straight*? Not to mention their measurements!"

Natural talent or no, he *really* didn't know if he could pull off the Great Wind Dancer Cook-Off!

Usually Sirocco looked to sweet Brisa, soothing Kona, and steady Sumatra to boost his confidence when it flagged.

But the fillies weren't there.

And he was invisible to Leanna and Sara, so *they* couldn't comfort him.

Which meant he had *no one*.

"I'm all alone in the world!" the colt neighed. "And more importantly, in the kitchen! What am I going to *do*?"

Before he could come up with an answer, Sirocco was distracted by a scuttling sound on the grass below him. He fluttered off the kitchen windowsill to have a look—and saw two scampering squirrels tussling over a pinecone.

Squirrels!

"How could I have forgotten?" Sirocco whinnied, his spirits lifting. "I'll go visit Gray the Squirrel. He built our apple tree house *and* he refereed our soccer competition. I bet he can help me with *my* big problem!"

With a happy nicker, Sirocco dashed to Gray's nest in an oak tree not too far away. When the colt arrived, he thrust his nose through Gray's kitchen window.

"Gray! You've got to help me!" Sirocco whinnied. "I'm nowhere *near* ready for the cook-off today!"

The plump squirrel was sitting at his kitchen table, eating acorns. He looked completely unsurprised to see Sirocco's horsy face poking into his house.

"Cook-off, eh?" Gray said. "I like the sound of that. Let me guess, it's you Wind Dancers against the four big horses, right?"

Gray was talking about Thelma, Fluff, Benny, and Andy, the giant, non-magic horses who lived in a paddock at the edge of the meadow.

Sirocco shook his head.

"Actually," he said, puffing out his chest, "I'm competing against Kona, Sumatra, and Brisa."

"A Wind Dancer competing against Wind Dancers?" Gray said, now frowning just a bit. "I *don't* like the sound of that."

Sirocco squirmed.

"It's just that, well, it turns out I'm this naturally talented chef," he explained. "But the fillies keep teasing me and . . ."

Sirocco trailed off lamely. Now that Gray had put him on the spot, it was kind of hard to remember why he *was* competing against his friends. But he pressed on anyway, hoping that Gray would see things his way.

"The truth is, I'm in a bind and I don't know how I can top the Awesome Apple Rutabaga Crunch I accidentally made this morning."

"*Pshaw,*" Gray said kindly, waving a paw at Sirocco. "You just need a little help from your friends!"

Sirocco thought about Kona, Brisa, and Sumatra. He felt a pang in his belly.

But he felt better when he saw that Gray was smiling at him.

"I'm your friend," the squirrel reminded him. "And I'm *also* a great cook, if not a 'naturally talented chef.'"

"That's true!" Sirocco remembered, cheering up. "You've always said that you make a mean Acorn Crunch Cake. But come to think of it, I've never tasted it."

"Well, I just happen to have my chief ingredient right here!" Gray offered, as he motioned to the pile of acorns on his table.

"Awesome!" Sirocco whinnied. "Gray, just tell me what to do!"

And the generous squirrel did just that.

He showed Sirocco how to crack the acorns under his heavy hooves.

He gave Sirocco a wire pastry cutter to clamp between his teeth. The tiny horse used it to mash butter and brown sugar together for the cake. Next, Gray had Sirocco add the acorns and bind all the ingredients together with pinesap!

"It's got a nice kick to it," Gray observed. "Much better than too-sweet honey or molasses."

"Oooo-kay," said Sirocco, who happened to *love* honey and molasses.

As he filled two baking pans with the chunky cake batter, the colt tried to shake off his uneasiness.

This is just what I wanted to cook, he reminded himself silently. *Something different from our same old appley, carroty,* horsy *meals. Right?*

Right! he answered himself with bravado.

But a half hour later—when the Wind Dancer and the squirrel pulled the cakes out of the oven—Sirocco couldn't help but wonder if he was, perhaps, *not* right.

And after Sirocco took his first taste of the Acorn Crunch Cake, it was all he could do not to neigh, *"Wrong!!!"*

Because clearly, painfully, crunchy, pine-sapped Acorn Crunch Cake was a dessert that only a *squirrel* could love!

"Mmmm," Gray exclaimed as he crunched and munched his way through his own

serving of cake. "Isn't this *great*?"

"It's, um," Sirocco said politely, "very . . . fragrant!"

Gray paused in his munching to stare at the colt.

"You *despise* Acorn Crunch Cake!" Gray declared. "You loathe it. You'd like to chuck it out the window to the woodchucks."

"No!" Sirocco neighed. He didn't want to insult his friend. But every word Gray had said was true, and Sirocco felt terrible about it—until he heard Gray laugh. The colt looked up in surprise.

"I don't know why you expected anything different," Gray chuckled. "This is *squirrelly* food. You're a *horse*!"

"But I'm a horse who's *supposed* to be a gourmet chef!" Sirocco complained. "How can I win the Great Wind Dancer Cook-Off without cooking something that's extra fabulously different?"

"Maybe you should focus more on fabulously delicious," Gray said sagely. Immediately, Sirocco imagined oatmeal muffins, carrot pudding, and apple brown Betty.

"Or maybe," Gray began, "you should focus *less* on . . ."

The squirrel trailed off.

"On what?" Sirocco pressed him.

"Well," Gray said, thoughtfully crunching his last bite of acorn cake, "why *do* you want to win this contest so badly? I mean, all four of you Wind Dancers like to eat the same foods—that is, food that *doesn't* taste like Acorn Crunch Cake—"

"—or gooseberries or dandelion greens or wild mushrooms, either, now that you mention it," Sirocco realized.

"Right," Gray agreed. "And what's more, Kona, Sumatra, and Brisa *are your friends*! Who cares who cooks, as long as the food is delicious and the meal is fun?"

"The *fillies* care," Sirocco said. He slumped sullenly against the kitchen table. "*They* want me to cook more often!"

"Well, how often *do* you cook?" Gray asked.

"Uh . . . never," Sirocco admitted.

Gray chuckled and grabbed Sirocco's barely touched Acorn Crunch Cake.

"Seems a shame," the squirrel mused between critter-crunchy bites. "After all, you Wind Dancers are a great team," Gray said with a shrug. "Usually, anyway!"

And that's when Sirocco realized something. All those belly pangs he'd been having that day? He'd *thought* they'd been for his friends' apple muffins and corn and carrot concoctions and berry pies.

But maybe they'd also been for his *friends*.

"Gray," Sirocco said, grinning at the squirrel, "I've got to go!"

"Where are you off to?" Gray asked, as Sirocco fluttered into the air.

"I've got a new recipe," Sirocco declared, aiming for home, "that I just *must* try!"

CHAPTER 6

The Great Wind Dancer
Cook-Off

The first thing Sirocco *heard* when he trotted through the apple tree house door was a burst of laughter from the kitchen.

The first thing he *felt* was a cozy warmth.

And the first thing he *smelled* was a delicious mix of apples, corn, and pie.

With a little shiver of happiness, Sirocco clip-clopped into the kitchen.

"You're here!" Brisa neighed. "Let the Great Wind Dancer Cook-Off begin!"

Sirocco scanned the dishes on the table. In addition to the tasty-looking pie Kona had made earlier, there was Brisa's pretty Pink Lady Apple soufflé, and Sumatra's bowl of buttery roasted corn.

"Those look pretty good," Sirocco said casually, trying to hide the gleam in his eye. "But wait until you see what *I'm* bringing to the cook-off!"

"Where is it?" Sumatra asked impatiently. "We've been *wondering* what you were planning!"

"It's not ready yet," Sirocco said simply.

"Not ready yet?" Kona neighed. "But Sirocco, *our* dishes are ready to go!"

"Mine will be worth the wait," Sirocco assured his friends.

"You see," Sirocco went on, pacing the kitchen floor, "a brilliant chef needs several things to make great food. . . ."

"Here we go again," Sumatra muttered, rolling her eyes at Kona and Brisa. "The great Sirocco speaks!"

Sirocco pretended not to hear. He pressed on.

"One of the things he needs," he said, "is natural talent, of course. Check! I've got that! Another thing is fabulous ingredients."

Sirocco fluttered over to the horses' pantry and threw open the doors. Inside, he saw oats and barley, corn and molasses, raisins and apples, carrots and parsnips, along with dozens of other wholesome ingredients.

They weren't exactly exotic foods.

But every last one of the ingredients was sure to make a horse happy!

"Check!" Sirocco declared.

"That's a change," Kona said. "I thought our ordinary horsy ingredients weren't good enough for you!"

"Wait, there's just one thing I'm missing," Sirocco went on. "The secret ingredient that makes every meal delicious!"

"What could that be?" Kona wondered, her violet-black eyes wide.

Sirocco stopped pacing.

He stopping tossing his mane around.

And he gave the fillies a smile as sweet as a sugar cube.

"He needs friends," Sirocco admitted. "Without them, he'll lose the cook-off, for sure!"

Sirocco had stunned the fillies several times that day. But none more than now.

"You're saying *you* need . . . *us*?" Brisa asked incredulously.

"Yup," Sirocco said.

"To do what?" Sumatra asked.

"What you've been doing all day," Sirocco replied. "Having fun cooking together while I . . ."

Sirocco paused to squirm. And Kona filled in his thought for him.

"While you spent your day being brilliant, but . . . lonely?"

Sirocco cringed. He didn't want to admit it. *Lonely?* Yes. *Brilliant?* Not so much!

So, he skirted Kona's question and simply said, "Who's ready to cook up a little surprise?"

Sumatra, Kona, and Brisa shot each other sidelong looks and tried to hide their teasing smiles.

Then Kona put on an earnest face and

said, "I'm ready. I couldn't be more ready!"

"Me, too!" Sumatra agreed, cheerfully clearing the fillies' cook-off dishes from the table so the horses would have room to work.

Brisa tied an apron around her neck to protect her pretty mane and said slyly, "Just tell us what to do, Chef Sirocco!"

The tiny colt trotted over to his pile of ingredients.

"Kona, why don't you combine some raisins, rutabaga, and maple syrup," Sirocco instructed.

Then he turned to Sumatra.

"Please mix up some molasses, cornmeal, and carrots," he requested.

"That's . . . different," Sumatra said skeptically as she gathered the ingredients.

"That's the point!" Sirocco said proudly. "Favorite ingredients, *new* combinations of them."

He scanned the remaining ingredients and gave Brisa parsnips, apples, honey, and bran.

And for himself, he chose oats, dates, sweet potatoes—and sugar cubes!

The four horses chuckled and chatted as they bustled around the kitchen. Brisa playfully flicked parsnip peels at Sirocco, and

Sirocco beaned each of the fillies with raisins when they weren't looking. By the time everyone had finished mixing up their ingredients, they were all laughing.

But with the fillies' work finished, it was time for Sirocco to go solo again. Grinning, he banished his fellow cooks from the kitchen.

A short (and very clattery) while later, Sirocco called to his friends: "Supper's on!"

The pretty fillies peeked curiously into the kitchen and saw that Sirocco had reset the table and laid out Kona's parsnip pie, Brisa's apple soufflé, and Sumatra's corn.

But there was no sign of *Sirocco's* dish other than a delicious smell coming from the oven.

"Let's eat!" Sirocco said. "I'm *starving*!"

Sirocco enjoyed the fillies' food so much, the other Wind Dancers could barely get a fork in edgewise!

As the horses feasted, they chattered happily.

"My pie is totally going to win the cook-off!" Kona announced confidently.

"What about the soufflé that I made?" Brisa retorted with a grin. "It was so pretty, I could hardly bear to de-puff it."

"Luckily, Sirocco did that for you," Sumatra said wryly. "Anyway, we *all* know that the roasted corn is the best—because it's the dish *I* cooked!"

To each of these boasts, Sirocco nodded happily.

"Your food *is* fabulous," he agreed, before adding, "but nothing's as good as dessert!"

Sirocco leapt up from the table and trotted to the oven. Carefully blocking the fillies' view, he pulled something out, then got busy putting some finishing touches on top of it.

"What are you up to?" Sumatra asked impatiently.

"Ooh, I can't wait to see!" Brisa added.

"Hold your horses, horses," Sirocco said. "It's a surprise. Specifically . . ."

Sirocco stepped aside to reveal a round, towering dish that looked just like a cake!

". . . the Sirocco Surprise!" the colt announced proudly.

The "cake" had four different layers— each made from the ingredients each horse had whipped together.

On top of the dessert was a puff of honeyed frosting. And this was dotted with ribbons, jewels, flowers, and butterflies—all carved from sparkling sugar cubes!

"It's *beauuuutiful*," Brisa breathed.

"And it actually smells *good*!" Sumatra

noted with more than a little surprise.

"It'll taste even better," Sirocco assured her. "What with my natural talent and all!"

Sirocco hoped his filly friends couldn't tell that he was holding his breath as Kona gripped a knife in her teeth and cut a nice large wedge out of the Sirocco Surprise.

Each of the Wind Dancers took a bite.

Initially, Sirocco tasted each lovely layer individually: first, the maple syrup/raisin/ rutabaga combo; next, the crispy corn-meal/carrot/molasses layer; then, the taste of parsnip/apple/honey and bran; and finally, the mixture of oats/dates/sweet potatoes and sugar cubes.

But then, all those flavors melded into one.

And Sirocco's whole mouth exploded with deliciousness!

One look at the fillies' stunned, blissful faces convinced the colt that they felt the same way about the Sirocco Surprise!

Sirocco's feet started tapping.

His wings started flapping.

And he launched into the victory dance he'd been dreaming about all day!

"*I'm* the winner!" he neighed. "I, Sirocco, have *won* the Great Wind Dancer Cook-Off! I'm the most *brilliant* chef in the dandelion meadow!"

"Wait a minute!" Sumatra protested (though she was licking frosting off her nose as she did). "Who declared *you* the winner?"

"All of us!" Sirocco said. "Our faces say it all. The Sirocco Surprise is the most delectable dish of the night!"

"It *is* dreamy," Brisa admitted.

"Brilliant, even," Sumatra grudgingly added.

"And it's so *different*," Kona pointed out, "even though it's full of all our usual favorite foods."

Sirocco was *just* about to whinny in victory, again, when Kona added, "But . . ."

"But?" Sirocco sputtered. "But what?!"

"But truthfully, Sirocco," Kona said gently, "we *all* made this cake together."

"So, how about a four-way tie?" Sumatra proposed, whipping one of her magic ribbons into a pretty bow.

"Or how about we just forget about winning and losing," Kona went on, "and finish our lovely meal?"

"Together!" Brisa declared.

Wearing serene smiles, the fillies looked to Sirocco, certain that he would agree.

"Sure, we made the Sirocco Surprise together, but it was *my* idea!" Sirocco burst out. "And you don't know what I *went through* to get there! I escaped vicious geese and poisonous mushrooms. I got lost in the woods and almost didn't make it out alive! Believe me—I have *suffered* for my art! I *deserve* to win."

Kona stifled a snort before getting serious and gazing at Sumatra and Brisa.

"He has a point," she said to them.

"He *does*?!" Sumatra gasped, while Sirocco grinned and resumed his victory dance.

"Sirocco is *indeed* a brilliant chef," Kona continued seriously. "And as our Cook-Off winner, he gets the privilege of making *all* our meals for, oh, at *least* the next week!"

"Um, what?" Sirocco said, putting his dance on pause to stare at Kona.

71

"Now, for breakfast tomorrow," Kona ordered the stunned colt, "I'd like some oatmeal pancakes."

"Oooh," Sumatra added with a grin, "and I'll take some fresh-pressed apple cider!"

"And for *lunch*," Brisa ordered with a giggle, "I'd *love* some carrot pasta."

"N-n-now hold on!" Sirocco stammered. "We never *talked* about this prize."

"I *know*!" Kona said with a mischievous grin. "This is *so* much better than a trophy, don't you think?"

"So, how about it?" Sumatra challenged the colt with a grin. "You ready to get busy in the kitchen?"

"But," Sirocco protested, "cooking with *you* guys was the whole *point* of the Sirocco Surprise. It was way more fun than cooking all by myself!"

Now it was the fillies who paused.

Immediately, they shifted from teasing—to touched. Brisa rushed to give Sirocco a nose nuzzle.

"We missed cooking with you today, too!" she declared. "It just *wasn't* the same without you making a big mess in the kitchen!"

"Exactly!" Sirocco replied, returning the nuzzle and grinning—a bit slyly. "I mean, what's *not* to love about cooking together? In the end, there's *less* work for everyone and *more* food! Especially for me!"

"Sirocco!" Sumatra scolded.

Sirocco cackled. But then he got (slightly) serious.

"Tell you what," he offered his friends, feeling only a *little* pang as he did. "How about we agree to share the work in the kitchen *and* the win for the Great Wind Dancer Cook-Off?"

Brisa, Kona, and Sumatra looked at each other and grinned. Then Kona turned to the colt and declared, "Deal!"

"And now," Sirocco said, happily trotting back to the table, "let's *seal* that deal with another piece of Sirocco Surprise!"

And a Tasty Good Night!

Later that evening, Sirocco once again found himself zipping through the air, thinking of food.

But this time, he wasn't alone.

Kona, Brisa, and Sumatra were with him. And so was a basket looped around his neck.

As the horses headed to Leanna and Sara's pretty yellow farmhouse, Sirocco pulled back the napkin covering the basket, and he and his friends peered inside one last time.

Nested inside were two fat slices of the Sirocco Surprise.

"They look so pretty!" Brisa said with satisfaction.

"And," Sirocco said smacking his lips, "they're made with ingredients both horses *and* little girls love!"

Reaching the farmhouse, Sirocco and the fillies landed on the kitchen windowsill. Then Sirocco carefully flew inside. He placed the basket with the two bedtime snacks—one each for Leanna and Sara—on the countertop. Then the happy horse rejoined his friends on the windowsill.

"I only wish I could be here," Sirocco said to the fillies, "when Leanna and Sara discover their treat and taste my brilliant cooking!"

"Not again!" Sumatra sputtered. "We *all* made the Sirocco Surprise together, you know that! Remember our *deal*?"

"Oh, right!" Sirocco said breezily. "Our deal. Okay, I *suppose* you can share the credit with me."

"*Sirocco!*" Now, it was Kona who was

sending a warning the colt's way.

"*Hello!*" Sirocco burst out with a belly laugh. "I'm *kidding*!"

"*Oh!*" Brisa said, blinking in surprise.

And to *Sirocco's surprise*, the fillies started giggling.

"C'mon, fellow chefs," Sirocco declared, fluttering off the windowsill. "Let's go home and have our leftover cake as a midnight snack. Because everybody knows that dessert shared with friends tastes the *sweetest* of all!"

Here's a sneak preview of *Wind Dancers* Book 9:

A Horse's Best Friend

CHAPTER 1
Puppy Love

"Heads up, Brisa!" the leader of the Wind Dancers called to the coral-pink filly as the tiny winged horses flew above their dandelion meadow. "Let's play ABC ball. Catch!"

Kona was holding a bright red Jolly ball between her front hooves.

"*Tra, la, la,*" Brisa warbled, as she bobbed with her head in the clouds.

"Come on!" Kona called to Brisa again.

"Why don't you throw the ball to me instead?" suggested Sirocco, the lone colt in the Wind Dancer foursome, as the sun glowed on his golden coat.

"ABC ball?" piped up sea-green Sumatra, the last of the Wind Dancers. "What's that?"

"We throw the ball to each other in alphabetical order, of course," Kona said primly. "Brisa goes first. She throws it to me, because K for Kona comes after B for Brisa. Then I'll throw the ball to Sirocco. And Sumatra, you get the ball last."

"What if I want to be first?" Sumatra demanded huffily.

"You can't," Kona said bossily. "SU-matra comes after SI-rocco. That's just the way it is!"

"Yeah, in *your* world, Miss Bossy-hooves!" Sumatra grumbled.

Kona frowned.

"I am—"

"—*not bossy!*"

Brisa and Sirocco had jumped in to finish Kona's sentence. Then they dissolved into giggles.

"Hey!" Kona said. She looked hurt, until Brisa swooped down to give her a nose nuzzle.

"Oh, don't feel bad," Brisa said. "We love you even if you *are* bossy!"

"And even if *I* don't necessarily want to play ABC ball," Sumatra added with a mischievous grin.

Kona was just about to say again how *not* bossy she was, when she heard something that stopped her.

It was a rustling, scampering sound.

Which was followed by a *yap-yap-yapping* sound.

And then by a round, furry critter bursting out of a thick clump of yellow dandelions!

The creature gazed up at the Wind Dancers with bright, brown eyes. He reared up on his hind legs and waved his front paws at the tiny flying horses. Then he lost his balance, and fell over in a heap.

"Oh!" Kona exclaimed, instantly forgetting her budding argument with her friends. "Look! It's a *puppy dog!*"

Continue the magical adventures with Breyer's

Let your imagination fly!

Sumatra

Sirocco

Kona

Brisa

BREYER®

Collect them all!